Mara's Long

Karene Turner

Illustrated by
Frances Espanol

To order additional copies of this book, contact:
Xlibris
1-800-455-039
www.xlibris.com.au
Orders@Xlibris.com.au

Illustrated by Frances Espanol

ISBN: Softcover   978-1-7960-0445-8
         EBook   978-1-7960-0444-1

Print information available on the last page

Rev. date: 08/12/2019

Mara's Long Hair

Written by

Karene Turner

Illustrated by **Frances Espanol**

Mara was a little girl not much bigger than you. She had lovely long brown hair that went down the middle of her back, big brown eyes, an upturned nose, a large mouth, and freckles on her cheeks. She lived with her mum in a house that had an upstairs and downstairs. The bedrooms were upstairs, and everything else was downstairs.

One morning she woke up to find that the sun was shining. It often did that, so that wasn't remarkable. Mara had been thinking about her hair. She liked having long hair, but she didn't like having to brush it. The brush nearly always found a tangle and pulled at her hair. Mum brushed it at night and plaited it, but it seemed to come out in the middle of the night and get knots in it.

"Mum, I've made up my mind. I'm not going to brush my hair today or ever again!" Mara called out down the stairs.

"I think we will have to talk about that," replied her mum.

Mara walked down the stairs in her pyjamas. She walked into the kitchen and sat down at the table. She poured cornflakes into her bowl and then added some milk. Then she started to eat her breakfast.

She suddenly felt a long stringy thing in her throat and started coughing. Mum came over, put she finger in Mara's mouth, and pulled out a long brown hair.

"You really will have to do your hair, Mara, so you don't swallow anymore of it!" Mum said. "Fetch the brush, and I'll do it."

Mara shook her head. "I don't want to do my hair today, Mum."

The phone rang, and Mum turned to where it lay on the bench and picked it up. "I would like you to brush your hair, or I will do it for you!" Mum replied as she pushed answer on the phone. "Hello there," Mum said into the phone.

Mara swung her hair behind her shoulders and continued to eat her breakfast. When she had finished, Mum was still talking on the phone, but she looked hard at Mara.

Mara got up and went back upstairs to her bedroom to get dressed. She was pulling her pyjama top off over her head when her hair got caught around a button. "Ow!" she cried. She tried to pull her pyjama top back on, but that hurt as well. She could hear Mum still talking on the phone. She grabbed her hair and put it behind her back. She then pulled her pyjama top off. This time it worked.

Mara then pulled on some tracksuit pants and a T-shirt, but she didn't brush her hair. She then went down the stairs and out the back door.

Mara grabbed an apple out of the basket Mum had near the back door, and then she got on her bicycle. With her hair streaming behind her, she rode very fast to the other end of the yard, where the big tree stood. She lay down under the tree to eat her apple.

A worm started to climb up her hair. A bird had been watching the worm. The bird flew down to eat the worm, and it got caught in Mara's hair. Then the wind blew up, and some of her hair got caught in the tree. Mara got scared. "Mum! Mum! Muuuum!" Mara yelled.

Mum came out the back door carrying a pair of scissors and hurried down to where Mara was yelling and the bird was squawking and the wind was blowing more of Mara's hair into the tree. Mum cut the hair that the bird had gotten stuck in. The bird flew away with the worm. Then Mum cut the hair that had gotten caught in the tree.

Mum then said, "I wish you had brushed your hair when I asked you too." Mum then took Mara's hand, and they headed back inside. Mum brushed Mara's hair. There were now long bits and short bits of hair. "Oh dear! We will have to go to the hairdresser to get your hair all one length!" Mum stated. Mum put Mara's hair into ponytails and rang the hairdresser.

At the hairdresser's, Mara had to sit in a really tall chair. The lady snipped and snipped at Mara's hair till Mara didn't think she was going to stop. Eventually she did, and by then Mara's hair came to her shoulders.

Mara always brushed her hair every day after that.

CPSIA information can be obtained
at www.ICGtesting.com
Printed in the USA
BVHW091223190819
556213BV00003B/39/P